DIAL BOOKS FOR YOUNG READERS

A division of Penguin Young Readers Group • Published by The Penguin Group
Penguin Group (USA) Inc., 375 Hudson Street, New York, NY 10014, U.S.A.

Penguin Group (Canada), 90 Eglinton Avenue East, Suite 700, Toronto, Ontario, Canada M4P 2Y3 (a division of Pearson Penguin Canada Inc.) • Penguin Books Ltd, 80 Strand, London WC2R 0RL, England • Penguin Ireland, 25 St. Stephen's Green, Dublin 2, Ireland (a division of Penguin Books Ltd) • Penguin Group (Australia), 250 Camberwell Road, Camberwell, Victoria 3124, Australia • (a division of Pearson Australia Group Pty Ltd) • Penguin Books India Pvt Ltd, 11 Community Centre, Panchsheel Park, New Delhi - 110 017, India • Penguin Group (NZ), Cnr Airborne and Rosedale Roads, Albany, Auckland 1310, New Zealand (a division of Pearson New Zealand Ltd) • Penguin Books (South Africa) (Pty) Ltd, 24 Sturdee Avenue, Rosebank, Johannesburg 2196, South Africa • Penguin Books Ltd, Registered Offices: 80 Strand, London WC2R 0RL, England
The publisher does not have any control over and does not assume any responsibility for
author or third-party websites or their content.

27

Library of Congress Cataloging-in-Publication Data
THE LITTLE RED HEN / Jerry Pinkney.
p.   cm.
Summary: A newly illustrated edition of the classic fable of the hen who is forced to do all the work of
baking bread and of the animals who learn a bitter lesson from it.
ISBN 978-0-8037-2935-3
[1. Folklore.] I. Pinkney, Jerry, ill. II. Little red hen. English.
PZ8.1.L72 2006   398.24'528625—dc22   2005013301

The full-color artwork was prepared using graphite, ink, and watercolor on paper.

To Atha Tehon

The **little red hen** greeted the sun
with a cheery "Good morning!"
It was going to be another busy day.

While hunting for worms and berries for her young ones, she came upon some strange seeds. Ever so carefully she scooped them up, then headed home.

On the way she greeted her neighbors, the **short brown dog**, the **thin gray rat**, the **tall black goat**, and the round pink pig. "I found these seeds," she said. "Can any of you tell me what they are?"

"They're wheat seeds," said one of the animals. "If you plant them, they'll grow into wheat for baking bread."

"Who will help me plant these seeds?"
asked the little red hen.
"Not I," said the rat.
"Not I," said the goat.
"Not I," said the pig.

"Surely you will," the little red hen
said to the dog. "You are so fond of digging."
"Not I," said the dog.

"Very well then," said the little red hen, "I will plant them myself." She dug holes in the ground and dropped the seeds in. A very busy hen was she!

Every day the little red hen scratched for food to feed her young ones. She also found time to care for the seedlings. She and her chicks watched as the wheat grew strong and ripe. "It is now time for harvesting," said the little red hen.

"Who will help me cut and thresh the wheat?"
asked she.

"Not I," said the **goat**.

"Not I," said the pig.

"Not I," said the **dog**.

"Surely you will," the little red hen said to the rat.
"You can use your tail to chop it easily."
"Not I," said the rat.

"Very well then, I will do it myself," said the little red hen. After snipping the stalks with her beak, she separated the grain with her claws. A very busy hen was she!

"Who will help me take the grain to the mill?" asked the little red hen.

"Not I," said the pig.

"Not I," said the dog.

"Not I," said the rat.

"Surely you will," the little red hen said to the goat. "You are strong and steady, and it's a lovely day to take out your cart."

"Not I," said the goat.

"Very well then," said the little red hen. "I will do it myself." So she fetched her shawl, then trudged off to the mill.

Mr. Miller ground her grain into flour and even gave her a jar of berry jam. The little red hen thanked him and began her long trek home.

"Who will help me bake the bread?" asked the little red hen.

"Not I," said the dog.

"Not I," said the rat.

"Not I," said the goat.

"Surely you will," the little red hen said to the pig. "It won't take much effort at all, and you are always delighted with my cooking."

"Not I," said the pig.

"Very well then," said the little red hen. "I will do it myself." She mixed the flour with yeast, salt, and water, then kneaded the dough, shaped it into a loaf, and put it into the oven. At last the bread was done.

As the little red hen took the hot loaf out of the oven, a tasty aroma circled the barnyard.

"I know who will eat the golden bread," said the little red hen.

"I surely will," said the **short brown dog**.

"I surely will," said the **thin gray rat**.

"I surely will," said the **tall black goat**.

"I surely will," said the round pink pig.

"Oh no you won't," said the little red hen. "You did not help me plant the seeds, nor thresh the wheat, nor take the grain to the miller, nor bake the bread.

"My chicks and I will eat it," clucked the little red hen. She set the table for herself and her family, cut the warm, soft bread, then spread sweet berry jam on each slice. **Oh joy of joys!**